Snowboarding Diary

by June Stratford and Jane Morrison

Illustrations by Celina Mosbauer

Photographs by Bill Thomas

PM Library
Emerald Nonfiction

U.S. Edition © 2013 HMH Supplemental Publishers
10801 N. MoPac Expressway
Building #3
Austin, TX 78759
www.hmhsupplemental.com

Text © 2001 Sue Bursztynski
Illustrations © 2001 Cengage Learning Australia Pty Limited
Originally published in Australia by Cengage Learning Australia

15   1957   16
4500630503

Text: Sue Bursztynski
Photographs: Bill Thomas
Printed in China by 1010 Printing International Ltd

Snowboarding Diary
ISBN 978 0 76 357457 4

Contents

Day 1 Jasmine Arrives

Dear Diary,

Today Mom and I picked up my friend, Jasmine, from the airport. I met Jasmine when my family went to Jamaica for a vacation, and we've been writing to each other ever since. Now Jasmine has come to spend some time with us. Mom and Dad are taking us snowboarding in the mountains.

Jasmine and I don't know how to snowboard, but we are both good skateboarders. Some of my friends at school say that snowboarding is just like skateboarding. I hope it is.

It's great to see Jasmine again!

"WOW!"

Jasmine has never seen snow before. In Jamaica, it is hot for most of the year. Jasmine is curious to see snow and I wonder what she'll think of it.

Jasmine and I were very excited to see each other at the airport. We couldn't stop talking all the way home in the car.

We checked out snowboards in a magazine. They are the same shape as skateboards but thinner, and of course they don't have any wheels. Maybe we will be good at snowboarding, too!

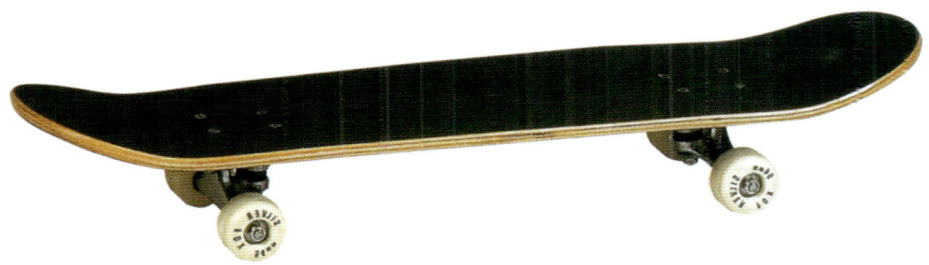

When we got home from the airport, we went to the park to practice our skateboarding. Jasmine is fantastic! She has great balance, and I think she'll learn how to snowboard very easily.

Gearing Up to Go!

This morning, we rented our snowboarding gear. We had great fun choosing clothes that are waterproof and not too tight. The jackets and pants have extra padding on the elbows, knees, and bottom because snowboarders often fall over—and we expect to do a lot of that!

We also rented helmets to protect our heads, and ski gloves to keep our hands warm. We chose colorful goggles, too. You need a lot of gear for this sport.

helmet

gloves

goggles

pants

boots

6

Our boots lace up around the ankle for support, and our snowboards are fitted with bindings that hold the boots tightly in place. We had to decide which foot was most comfortable on the front of the snowboard. I chose the left. A strap attaches the board to your leg, so if your feet come out of the bindings, the snowboard won't slide away.

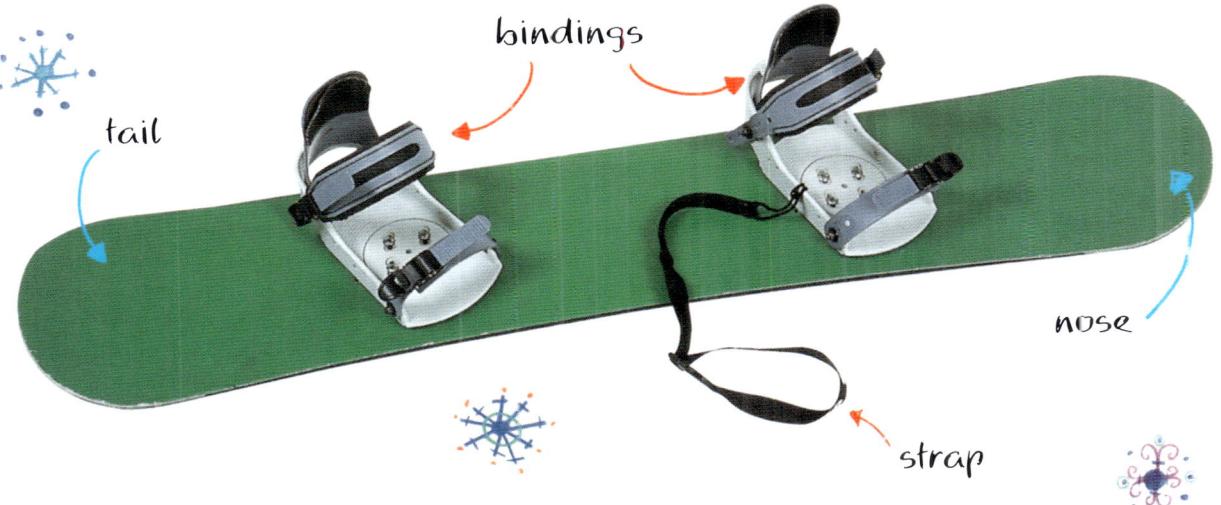

bindings

tail

nose

strap

All snowboards are made from flexible wood. The wood bends and makes snowboarding easier when jumping and turning. The nose and tail of the snowboards are turned up slightly. This is so the boards won't dig into the snow and get stuck.

This afternoon, after a few hours traveling, we reached the winding road up to the mountains. Snow began to fall, and Dad had to drive very carefully on the icy roads.

We finally got to the lodge where we are staying. Jasmine and I jumped out of the car so that we could feel the snow. Jasmine couldn't believe how white everything looked and how cold and hard the snow felt.

I made a snowball and threw it at Jasmine. She laughed and threw one back. I ducked, but she still got me!

A snowboarding competition for beginners is being held on Saturday. Jasmine and I want to be in it. I only hope I can snowboard by then!

Beginners Snowboard Competition

Saturday 5 PM

Come and show off what you've learned in your snowboarding lessons!

Day 3

Snowboarding Lesson

It takes a while to get all this gear on.

Jasmine and I put on our snowboarding gear after breakfast. Then we rushed up to the nursery slopes where we were taking snowboarding lessons.

A lot of snow had fallen overnight. We saw some snowboarders. They looked fantastic! This deep powder snow is soft enough to fall on and not too slippery to control the board.

9

This is Sarah, our instructor. She is an experienced snowboarder. There are five of us in the class, and Sarah said that safety was the first thing we all had to learn. She handed out this safety checklist:

Safety Rules for Snowboarding

1. Always snowboard in groups.

2. Stay away from trees.

3. Let someone know where you are going and what time you expect to return.

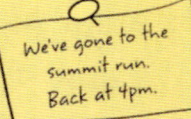

We've gone to the summit run. Back at 4pm.

4. Keep clear of others on the slopes and always be polite.

Then Sarah gave us step-by-step instructions:

GETTING STARTED

1. Fit one boot into the front binding.

2. Fasten the toe and ankle safety straps.

3. Try standing up—it's easy!

4. When you can stand, push forward with the other foot.

5. Practice with both feet in the bindings but only when you are successful with one foot.

STOPPING

1. Turn the board sideways across the mountain.

2. Lean heavily on the uphill edge. This movement acts like a brake.

Even Sarah falls over sometimes!

FALLING OVER

Sarah said that all snowboarders fall over.

We had fun learning how to fall over safely. We fell on our knees and arms to protect our wrists and hands. I was very good at falling over!

Sarah taught us how to do toe turns and heel turns. She gave us this diagram so we could remember her instructions.

TURNING

1. To do a toe turn, push the board on the edge that is nearest to your toes. As the left foot is in front here, this is a right turn.

2. To turn left, do a heel turn. Push the board on the edge that is nearest to your heel.

Toe turn

Heel turn

For the rest of the day, Jasmine and I practiced all we had learned, and even made progress. We hope we'll be ready for the competition, which is on Saturday.

Tomorrow, we hit the big slopes!

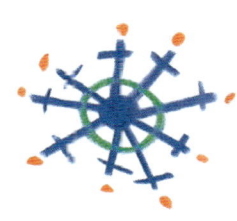

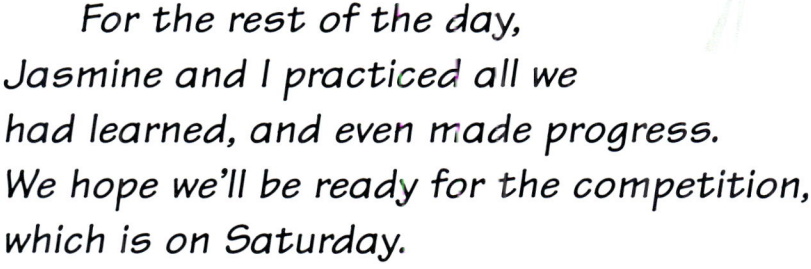

Day 4
Practice Makes Perfect

Sarah took our class up the mountain today. Jasmine and I were excited to get on the chairlift. We waited at the loading station. Looking over our shoulders, we saw the chairlift getting closer. The attendant helped us sit down with our snowboards pointing up the mountain. It was a bit scary, because you have to hop on the chairlift while it's moving.

This is HIGH!

Children's Lift Ticket

A

P

№ 217729

The view from the chairlift was fantastic. The next thing we knew, we were at the top. Standing up, we slowly slid away from the moving chairlift. It was easier than I thought it would be, now that I can balance on my snowboard.

Sarah led the way. We had to remember all the things she had taught us.

We zigzagged down the slope, using heel-and-toe turns. It was great fun.

Suddenly, I started going very fast and felt out of control. Throwing myself forward, I tried to fall so I didn't get hurt. I rolled over and pulled my board back by the strap.

I looked up and saw Jasmine hurtling straight toward me. I tried to move, but she landed on top of me with a great thump. We were so tangled up we couldn't move.

Sarah had seen what happened and rushed down to us, followed by two members of the ski patrol. They untangled us and made sure we weren't hurt. Then Sarah asked them to take us back to our lodge. Sarah said we need to be more careful and remember Safety Rule 4.

Mom and Dad were very surprised to see us back at the lodge so soon. We explained what had happened and they were glad that we were all right.

Aaaah!
Hot Chocolate!

'No broken bones- Yippee!!'

Our muscles were sore and we were very cold. We both had hot showers and Dad made us some hot chocolate to cheer us up.

Snowboarding can be dangerous if you don't follow the safety rules. Mom said she was happy we didn't break any bones. So am I!

Day 5 Advanced Techniques

When I woke up this morning, I got out of bed very slowly and carefully. Jasmine said she had never felt so sore. I hope we will feel better soon. We don't want to miss the competition! The competitors have to start at the chairlift and snowboard down the easy slopes without falling over. The person with the fastest time wins.

Here we are, limbering up.

At the beginning of our lesson today, we did a lot of stretching to loosen our muscles. Then we practiced our turns. Sarah said we had to remember to lean forward for extra balance. This helps control the snowboard. Being in control of the snowboard gives you confidence.

By lunchtime we were all tired, so we watched the older snowboarders on the half-pipe. The half-pipe's surface is made from tightly packed snow.

We saw a boy on the half-pipe doing some amazing stunts. He did aerials, where he grabbed the board with one hand. He seemed to fly through the air. Another snowboarder rode the walls, turned upside down in the air, and still landed on his feet. I wish I could do stunts like that.

Stunts are all about speed, balance and center of gravity. Sarah told us it takes a lot of time and practice to learn these special tricks.

'Amazing!'

Day 6

The Big Competition

This morning, Jasmine and I woke up very excited about the competition. At ten o'clock, we met the other competitors at the chairlift. The organizer handed each of us a number to tie on our backs, and then the competition began.

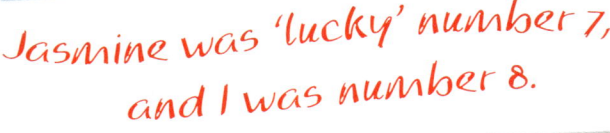

Jasmine was 'lucky' number 7, and I was number 8.

There was a big crowd watching, and Mom and Dad were there, too. I was nervous as I waited for my turn. I watched some of the others snowboard down the slope. There were lots of falls, but some competitors made it to the bottom.

Then it was Jasmine's turn. She didn't even look nervous! Jasmine pushed off from the top and was on her way. She looked great as she sped down the slope, turning from left to right using heel and toe turns. Jasmine was amazing, considering this was her first time on snow. And she made it to the finish line without falling over!

It was my turn next. I pushed off, balanced my weight in the middle of the board, and picked up speed. I was doing really well, my best yet. Coming toward the finish line, I hit a small mound of snow. I flew through the air and crash-landed. I was really disappointed. I had no chance of reaching the finishing line. At least I'd landed in soft snow, and I had a great time racing.

The prizes were presented after the competition. And guess what—Jasmine came in second! She was so excited when she showed me her medal. I am very proud of her.

It was time to go home. We packed up our gear and climbed into the car. Jasmine and I were so tired. Snowboarding was great fun and we had learned a lot in a short time.

It had been a terrific way to spend time with my friend. I looked across at Jasmine to speak to her, but she was fast asleep.

I hope she can come back next year.

The end!

23

Glossary

aerials	snowboarding stunts in the air
bindings	hold boots firmly in place on the snowboard
center of gravity	center of balance in an object
chairlift	bench seats that hang from a long cable, which is driven by a motor. It carries people up the mountain
loading station	a place where people board a chairlift
nursery slopes	gradual slopes where beginners learn
strap	a strap that attaches the snowboard to the ankle